Kathy Stinson · Dušan Petričić
The Dance of the Violin

annick press
toronto + berkeley + vancouver

We acknowledge the support of the Canada Council for the Arts and the Ontario Arts Council, and the participation of the Government of Canada/la participation du gouvernement du Canada for our publishing activities.

Library and Archives Canada Cataloging in Publication

Stinson, Kathy, author
    The dance of the violin / Kathy Stinson ; Dušan Petričić.

Issued in print and electronic formats.
ISBN 978-1-55451-900-2 (hardback).—ISBN 978-1-55451-901-9 (epub).—
ISBN 978-1-55451-902-6 (pdf)

    1. Bell, Joshua, 1967- —Juvenile fiction. I. Petričić, Dušan, illustrator II. Title.

PS8587.T56D36 2017   jC813'.54   C2016-905507-8

Published in the U.S.A. by Annick Press (U.S.) Ltd.
Distributed in Canada by University of Toronto Press.
Distributed in the U.S.A. by Publishers Group West.

Printed in China

Visit us at: www.annickpress.com
Visit Kathy Stinson at: www.kathystinson.com
Visit Joshua Bell at: www.joshuabell.com

Also available in e-book format. Please visit www.annickpress.com/ebooks.html for more details. Or scan

To artists of all ages everywhere, striving for the stars—through words, pictures, movement, and music.
—K.S.

To my grandchildren Lara, Rastko, Andrej, Katarina, Irma, and Uroš: Please, never give up!
—D.P.

From the time he was very young, Joshua loved making music. He drummed on pots. He trumpeted into cardboard tubes.

After his parents found him strumming
elastic bands, they bought him a violin.

When he played his first song, a twinkling star appeared above his head.

When he learned other songs, whole stories poured from his violin.

One day Joshua rushed home from his music lesson. "Mom! Dad! I have to go to Kalamazoo."

"What's in Kalamazoo?"
"A competition! The winner gets to perform with *an orchestra!* Imagine *me* playing with a *whole orchestra!*"

Joshua showed his teacher the
music he wanted to learn.
The teacher shook his head.
"This is a very difficult piece,
even for adults."
"But I love it. It's soft and it's
loud, it's fast and—"
"And this is your *first*
competition."
"I hear a *story* in it—about
dancers being chased by a bear.
A bear! Their ship gets lost at
sea! I have to learn this piece!"

"In that case, Joshua, let's begin."

Practicing the tricky fingering made Joshua's hand sore, but he was determined to get it right. He especially liked playing very fast. *Prestissimo!*

"Slow ... down ... slow ... down," his teacher said.

The metronome helped Joshua play *adagio*.
Tick … tock … tick … tock … tick … until,
weeks later, he got all the notes just right and
was ready to speed up. *Tick tock tick tock.*

The day before the competition, Joshua's parents drove him to Kalamazoo. For five long hours he practiced his music in his head. By the time they arrived at their hotel, Joshua's insides felt the way his violin sounded if the strings were tuned too tight.

That night he dreamt he was onstage and flubbed a switch from the E chord to the G. The audience laughed. *Hahahahahahaha!*

"Don't worry," his dad said. "Everyone gets nervous before a competition."

"No matter what happens," his mom said, "just remember how much you love that music."

Waiting for his turn to play, Joshua shifted nervously on his chair. He twiddled a loose thread on his shirt. He wiped his sweaty hands on his sleeves.

The music one student played tickled every hair on Joshua's head and vibrated right down to his toes. Another student hit all the right notes, but they hung limp in the air like wet laundry on a clothesline.

"Next up, Joshua Bell."

Joshua walked onto the stage and lifted
his violin into position under his chin.
He held his bow lightly, but not too lightly.
He carefully placed his fingers on the strings.
His parents smiled. The judge nodded.
And Joshua began to play.
Almost right away—*scree*—a small
mistake. Hardly noticeable.
He kept going.

Then his fingers
stumbled. His bow
stuttered. The notes
wobbled and—*splat!*—
out tumbled a dancer,
flat on her face.

Joshua stopped playing.
The judge sighed.
The competition was over.
Joshua turned to leave the stage. But—

"I'd really like to start over."

The judge furrowed his brow.
"All right."

Joshua took a deep breath and let it out.
Again he placed his violin under his chin.
Again he raised his bow.

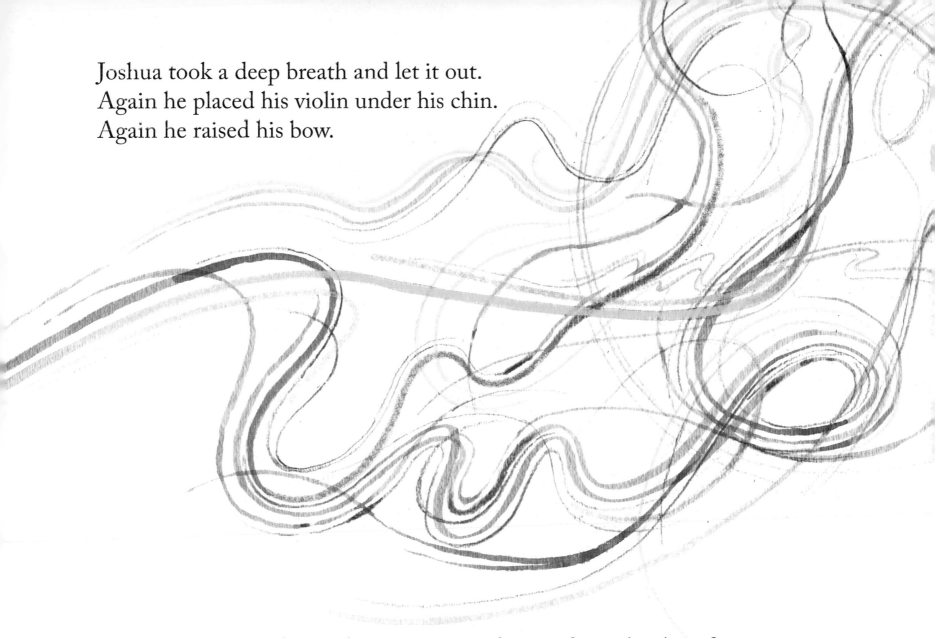

Inside his head, two dancers appeared, poised to take their first steps.
He drew his bow across the strings and two more dancers appeared.

Soon the notes spilling from the violin were pushing and pulling a whole roomful of dancers here and there, this way and that. Red skirts swirled and black boots twirled. The dancers flung each other dizzily around and around the room until Joshua felt dizzy too.

One final note, one final swoop, and Joshua knew—
from every hair on his head to the very tips of his toes—
that he had played better than ever before.

His dancers circled round. One winked. One kissed his cheek. Then they lifted Joshua high and higher still, till he could almost touch the stars.

Is Joshua a real boy?

He was. Joshua Bell is a grown man now and one of the finest classical violinists in the world. You can learn more about his musical career at joshuabell.com.

Did Joshua Bell really make a huge mistake at a competition?

Yes. He was only twelve years old when he entered the Stulberg International String Competition for the first time. The music he chose to play, Édouard Lalo's *Symphonie Espagnole,* has been famous among violinists for being difficult to master ever since it was first performed in 1875.

Did Joshua Bell really stop playing, then ask if he could start again?

He did. No one had told him what to do if he made a serious mistake. Having lost his confidence he might have played badly, but knowing he had nothing to lose he ended up playing better than he ever had.

Did he win the competition that day?

He came in third, a remarkable achievement for someone so young, playing such a difficult piece, and with points against him for his mistake. He did go on to win plenty of other competitions though, including this one the very next year.

Like everyone else, Joshua Bell still makes mistakes onstage sometimes. And when he does, he remembers that day when focusing on his love of music, rather than trying so hard to play perfectly, helped him play his very best.